Posey,
the
class Pest

Daisy DREAMER

Posey, the Class Pest

By Holly Anna • Illustrated by Genevieve Santos

LITTLE SIMON
New York   London   Toronto   Sydney   New Delhi

LITTLE SIMON

An imprint of Simon & Schuster Children's Publishing Division
1230 Avenue of the Americas, New York, New York 10020
First Little Simon hardcover edition July 2018
Copyright © 2018 by Simon & Schuster, Inc.
Also available in a Little Simon paperback edition.
All rights reserved, including the right of reproduction in whole or in part in any form.
LITTLE SIMON is a registered trademark of Simon & Schuster, Inc., and associated colophon is a trademark of Simon & Schuster, Inc. For information about special discounts for bulk purchases, please contact Simon & Schuster Special Sales at 1-866-506-1949 or business@simonandschuster.com. The Simon & Schuster Speakers Bureau can bring authors to your live event. For more information or to book an event contact the Simon & Schuster Speakers Bureau at 1-866-248-3049 or visit our website at www.simonspeakers.com.
Designed by Laura Roode
Manufactured in the United States of America 0618 FFG
2 4 6 8 10 9 7 5 3 1
Library of Congress Cataloging-in-Publication Data
Names: Anna, Holly, author. | Santos, Genevieve, illustrator.
Title: Posey, the class pest / by Holly Anna ; illustrated by Genevieve Santos.
Description: First Little Simon paperback edition. | New York : Little Simon, 2018. | Series: Daisy Dreamer ; #7 | Summary: When Daisy Dreamer's imaginary friend Posey joins her at school, he nearly ruins the group project she and her friends are working on although he is trying to be helpful.
Identifiers: LCCN 2017047479 | ISBN 9781534412705 (eBook) | ISBN 9781534412682 (pbk) ISBN 9781534412699 (hc)
Subjects: | CYAC: Imaginary playmates—Fiction. | Magic—Fiction. | Schools—Fiction. | Friendship—Fiction. | Video games—Fiction. | BISAC: JUVENILE FICTION / Imagination & Play. | JUVENILE FICTION / Humorous Stories. | JUVENILE FICTION / Readers / Chapter Books.
Classification: LCC PZ7.1.A568 Pos 2018 (print) | DDC [Fic]—dc23
LC record available at https://lccn.loc.gov/2017047479

CONTENTS

Chapter One

Sweet Dreams!

"Sweet dreams, Daisy Dreamer!" Mom and Dad say as they turn off the lights.

"Wait! I'm not *tired*!" I tell them, but the door clicks shut. I stare up at the glow-in-the-dark stars on my ceiling and yawn.

Then I hear a familiar voice. "I'm not tired either!"

I squint my eyes to see in the dark.

I wish I were a cat, like Sir Pounce, so I could have super-duper night vision.

"Posey?" I call out. "Is that you?" My heart is beating so thumpety fast. Then I spy a light tracing a new imaginary door on my wall. The door swings open, and there's my imaginary friend, wearing a big silly grin on his face.

"Hi, Daisy!" he says.

I breathe a sigh of relief. "You scared me!"

He slaps his knee and laughs, like he thinks that's so funny. "Sorry. I heard you weren't tired. So, do you want to have an adventure?"

I open my mouth, and another *big fat* yawn rolls out. "Isn't it kind of late to start an adventure?" I ask.

Posey jumps onto my bed. "Not in the WOM!" he says.

The WOM is the World of Make-Believe. *Obviously.*

"We could go to Roller-Coaster Raceway!" Posey suggests. "Or Bouncy Town, which is a whole town made out of bounce houses!"

I get up on one elbow. That *does* sound fun . . . but my eyes feel *so* heavy. . . .

"And you'd love the Pet Post Office!" Posey cheers. "It's a post office completely run by dogs, cats, guinea pigs, and more!"

I flop back down on my pillow.
"Maybe tomorrow . . . ," I say through
another yawn. "I'm totally zonked."

Posey shakes my arm. "But you
said you weren't tired."

I pull my arm back and shut my eyes. "I know, but I'm so sleepy now. Plus I have school tomorrow." Now I can feel myself fading fast.

"May *I* go to school with you?" Posey asks.

I snuggle deeper into my pillow. "Sure, Posey. Whatever you say," I murmur, before falling completely and totally asleep.

☆ Chapter Two ☆

Stowaway

Mr. Roberts slaps me five as I walk into the classroom. I say hi to Jasmine and Lily, my two best friends. Then I unzip my bag and unload my school stuff.

"Good morning, my candy-scented pencils!" I say because I'm really happy to see them. "Good morning, my rainbow unicorn notebook! And good morning, Posey. . . . Wait, *Posey?!*"

I cover my backpack before anyone sees him, but it's too late. Jasmine and Lily come right over.

"Wait! Is that who I think it is?" Jasmine asks.

"I saw him too!" Lily adds.

I put a finger to my lips.

"*Shh,*" I say. Then we gather around my backpack so nobody can see—and I open it again.

"HI, GUYS!" Posey shouts. All three of us squeal. How did my goober imaginary friend cram his entire imaginary self into a kid-size backpack?

"What are you doing here?" I whisper.

Posey looks confused. "Last night you said I could come to school with you!"

Hmm, I do not remember saying that at all, but I was very tired. "Posey, you can't come to *school*."

His smile vanishes. Posey sticks out his lower lip, and boy, do I feel like a big meanie. *Obviously.*

"Okay, okaaay," I whisper. "But you have to *promise* to behave! And you have to stay *invisible*!"

Posey leaps out of my backpack and cries, "I PROMISE!"

Then he sits in my chair. Jasmine and Lily try not to laugh. I sigh and

put my backpack and lunch box in my cubby. Gabby is there too. She gives me a sideways glance.

"You're weird sometimes," she says.

I finish shoving my stuff into my cubby. "Why?"

"Because I saw you talking to your *backpack*," she says, like it's a crime or something.

I laugh because that's the most preposterous thing I've ever heard.

"I was not!" I say. *I was talking to someone* inside *my backpack*. But she doesn't need to know that.

Gabby scowls. "You're up to some-thing, Daisy Dreamer, and I'm going to find out what."

Oh, no, you're not! I say in my head. *Because I am too smart for that!*

A Close Call

"It's Team Report time!" Mr. Roberts announces after attendance. "I'm going to divide you into groups, and each team will present a report."

Jasmine, Lily, and I get to be on the same team. I think it's because we all crossed fingers at the same time.

"Today the report will be on video games!" our teacher goes on. "And part of your grade will be how well you work as a team."

Oh yay! I think. *I love video games.* Plus we are a perfect team, so of course we'll work well together! *Obviously.*

Lily, Jasmine, and I all sit at our team table, with Posey in the middle.

"We're going to *crush* this report!" Jasmine says.

Posey scratches his head. "Why would we want to crush it?" he asks. "Oh, and what is a video game?"

Jasmine and Lily snort-laugh.

"It's a game you play on your TV or computer," Lily explains. "It's like a story, and you get to be a player in the story."

Posey points to himself and Jasmine nods. "Yes, *you!*" she says. "And you can do just about *anything* in a video game. You can even win stuff!"

But Posey still doesn't understand. "Why don't you just play the game in real life?"

"Because!" I whisper-shout. "Not everybody can visit the World of Make-Believe, so this is like the next best thing! I promise, video games are fun. So can we dream up some ideas already?"

Lily goes first. "Let's have our game be about fairies!"

I roll my eyes because of course Lily wants a fairy video game. "Fairies are fine, but I was thinking our game should be about *skateboards*!"

Then Jasmine sighs loudly. "Fairies
and skateboards are so *bor*-ing. Our
game should be about stuffed animals.
They *never* go out of style."

Then I stand up because I have to
stick up for what I like.

"Skateboards are *cool*!" I say.

Then Lily stands up. "Well, fairies are *magical*!"

Now Jasmine gets up. "And stuffed animals are *adorable*!"

Everything is getting totally out of control—until Posey holds his hand up like a stop sign.

"I have an idea," he says. "Why not make a game about a fairy who rides a flying skateboard to save a bunch of stuffed animals?"

We all look at one another and smile because that is not a bad idea. It is not a bad idea at all! Then Posey snaps his fingers. And—*POOF!*—a fairy on a skateboard with a stuffed animal

appears in the middle of our table! We quickly block the skateboarding fairy so no one will see.

"*Posey!*" I whisper desperately. "You can't do magic in the classroom!"

Posey shrugs. "Okay, fine. Have it *your way!*" He snaps his fingers again and the fairy disappears.

As we plop back down onto our seats, my heart is hammering against my ribs. I scan the classroom to make sure no one saw anything. Luckily, everyone is busy working on their own projects. *Phew!*

That was *way* too close.

CHAPTER FOUR

The Glitter-Litter Incident

"Okay. We have a fairy on a skateboard and stuffed animals," I say, trying to get us back on track.

Jasmine and Lily nod.

"And where should our story take place?" Lily asks.

I pick up my pencil and start to write everything down. "Probably in an imaginary world since we don't have fairies in the real world."

Posey gives that idea two big thumbs-up.

"And are the fairies nice?" Jasmine asks.

Lily sighs heavily. "Of course they're nice!" she says. "They're fairies."

I quickly write down *nice fairies*.

"What about the skateboards?" I ask. "Should we make them *alive*?"

Jasmine gives me a funny look. "How can a skateboard be *alive*?"

I flick my pencil down. "A skateboard can be alive if it's magical."

I can tell that Jasmine thinks this is too weird because she huffs. "Let's just make the skateboard able to fly all by itself—like a magic carpet. So it's magic but not alive."

"Fine," I say, feeling a little grumpy. And for the sake of finishing the project, I let it go. Then we all agree the fairy is saving the stuffed animals from a giant named Rewdus. Rewdus wants to keep all the stuffed animals for himself. Then I sketch a picture of Rewdus.

"He needs a bigger nose and sharper teeth!" Posey directs. "He's a giant. He has to be scary!"

I erase the nose and draw a larger one. That's when I see Carol and Gabby leaning over from another table and spying on us!

"Hey! NO PEEKING!" I shout at them. "That's cheating!"

Mr. Roberts hears me yelling and comes over. "Is there a problem, girls?"

Gabby and I both shake our heads.

"Okay," Mr. Roberts says, "then let's get back to work."

As Gabby turns back to her team's table, Posey slips something into her pink pencil bag. Then a foxlike grin spreads across his face.

"Posey, what did you just do?" I ask.

Posey rocks back and forth.

"Oh nothing," he says innocently. "I just put a little glitter-litter in Gabby's bag. The next time she opens it, she's in for a sparkly surprise!"

My eyes bug out. "Posey! You can't do that!"

Quickly I sneak over to try and remove the glitter-litter from Gabby's bag while she's not looking. That's when things get messy.

POP-BANG-BOOM!

The glitter-litter explodes all over me. I look like a disco ball. Then the whole class breaks out laughing and Mr. Roberts runs back over. *Uh-oh.*

"I'm so sorry!" I tell him. "I only meant to use a little glitter for our game."

But instead of getting me in really big trouble, the shiny mess makes Mr. Roberts laugh. "It's all right, Daisy.

Just clean yourself up and get back to work."

Wow, that was another close one, I think as I brush off the glitter over the wastebasket.

Posey floats over and asks if he can help. That's when I *taste* the glitter. It is even *in* my mouth. Yuck!

"No, thank you," I say in my calm voice. "You've helped enough already."

CHAPTER Five

Lunchtime Disaster

BBBRRRRRRING-A-DING-A-DING!

The lunch bell rings, and wow, do we need a break.

I sure hope things get better after lunch because they couldn't get any worse. After the glitter-litter bag, Posey broke the pencil sharpener, made (and destroyed) a tower of rulers, and let a squirrel into our classroom.

Jasmine laughs. "Wow! That squirrel wouldn't stop chasing Carol. Gabby must have screamed the whole time!"

This gets Lily going. "Oh, and poor Mr. Roberts almost slipped *twice* trying to shoo that little squirrel back out the window!"

Posey frowns. "I really thought the squirrel was a student. He looked ready to learn."

Posey can't understand why animals don't go to school. I keep telling him that only kids go to school in the real world—not animals. But whenever I say the word "kids," it makes Posey giggle. That's because he thinks I mean *baby goats*. I quickly correct myself again.

"I meant only *human* kids go to school," I say. "Not baby goats!"

Jasmine puts her arm around Posey. "Come on. Let's get lunch. A little food might help our mood."

Posey hops to his feet. "Okay! I'll meet you there. I just have to grab something!"

My friends and I sit at our usual table for lunch. Posey comes through the door with a giant brown bag.

"Whoa, what did you bring for lunch?" Lily asks.

Then Posey smiles and cries out, "FRIENDS!"

As soon as he opens his bag, a bunch of crazy creatures fly out! Pretty Pixies, Cloud Critters, Golly Ghosts, Moonsters—you name it. It looks like all of the WOM is here, and they're hungry!

They grab trays and stand in the
lunch line. Oh no! This is beyond bad.
I jump up from my seat.

"Posey!" I cry. "Are you trying to get me kicked out of school?"

Posey laughs. "Of course not! My friends look like ordinary kids to all the real-world people. No one will notice!"

I hope he's right. But when I look around, all the real-world kids are asking questions like:

"Hey! Where'd all the new kids come from?"

"Do you think we are being invaded by another school?"

"Are we going to run out of pizza?"

I glare at Posey and clench my fists. "Your friends need to leave—now!"

He catches my drift and whistles loudly. The WOM group stampedes out of the cafeteria and onto the playground.

Hmm, that's not exactly what I meant!

Now the playground looks like a circus. The new kids are hogging all the slides, swings, and monkey bars. There's no room for the real-world kids to play!

"Daisy, you *have* to fix this," Jasmine says as an octopus-shaped Cloud Critter takes over the top of the monkey bars.

I grab Posey by the shoulders and shout, "Enough!"

Posey bats his eyes innocently and asks, "What's wrong? Isn't this what kids do at recess?"

"Yes!" I answer. "But this playground is for kids who go to *this* school!"

Posey rubs his chin thoughtfully. "That makes sense," he says. Then he pulls out his bag and invites his friends back inside.

Jasmine, Lily, and I groan. Then we head to the library to work on our project—in peace.

Chapter Six

Loopy Library

First we stop by our classroom to pick up everything we need for our project: colored pencils, markers, poster board, tape, and notecards. Then we hurry down the hall to the library.

It's so quiet there, you could hear a Pretty Pixie sneeze. We sit at a table beside an open window that is not facing the playground. Then we get

64

to work. I start coloring, and Jasmine looks at my drawing.

"Way too many skateboards," she grumbles.

Then Lily looks over and adds, "Yeah, who cares about skateboards, anyway?"

And of course this makes me mad because *I* care. *Obviously.*

But Lily ignores my angry face and keeps going. "Let's forget skateboards for now. We need to figure out the end

of the game. In my opinion, the fairies should save the stuffed animals from the giant."

Jasmine lets out a loud harrumph. "No way! The stuffed animals should definitely save the fairies from the giant."

Then Lily balls up her paper and throws it in the wastebasket.

"SHHHH!" Mrs. Page, the librarian, shushes us from behind her desk.

Jasmine plants her elbows on the table. "Maybe we should each do our *own* projects," she whispers grumpily. "Then at least *mine* will be good."

Lily folds her arms. "Excuse me, but mine will be better," she whisper-yells back.

I can't believe we're fighting again, but I agree. "Okay, fine! At least with my own video game I can have as many talking skateboards as I want! And they can be alive!"

We split up and go to different tables. I make a poster for *my* game. Lily writes a story for her game and Jasmine draws scenes for her game. That's when trouble walks in.

"*There* you are! I've been looking for you guys *everywhere*!" Posey says from the doorway.

I look at Mrs. Page for a reaction and then I remember she can't see or hear Posey. He is imaginary. *Obviously.*

The library is the last place Posey should be! Lily, Jasmine, and I pause. We are terrified of what might happen. Then he flies over with his arms flapping every which way like crazy. All that flapping kicks up a gust of wind that blows Lily's cards everywhere!

"Oopsies!" Posey says. He dances around, trying to catch the cards, and that's when a bag of imaginary friend dust falls out of his pocket and spills on Jasmine's work. Now her markers and pencils begin to draw by themselves.

"Quick, catch them before they ruin everything!" I shout.

We don't ever hear Mrs. Page shushing us because we're too busy trying to catch the pens and pencils before they rewrite all the books in the library!

Poor Jasmine has a yellow highlighter buzzing around her head like a bee. Lily and I barely hold on to the rest of the pens and pencils. The magic makes them rattle in our hands.

"GIRLS!" Mrs. Page shouts in a not-so-library-ish voice. "What in the world is going on?"

We stop and stare helplessly at Mrs. Page and then back at our projects. What a mess! Jasmine's shirt is flecked with yellow highlighter marks. My poster board has scribbles all over it. And Lily has pens sticking out of her hair like chopsticks.

"I'm going to have to ask you to leave the library," Mrs. Page says firmly.

So we collect our stuff and go into the hall, where we stare at one another in disbelief. We have zero, zilch, zip to show for our report.

Then the bell rings.

"We are in so much trouble," I say.

Lily and Jasmine both nod glumly.

Then Posey taps my arm and asks,
"Are you mad at me?"

And I laugh right out loud because
I'm not mad. I'm *furious*.

☆Chapter Seven☆

The Lecture

Mr. Roberts claps his hands to get the class's attention.

"Presentation time!" he announces. We split back into our groups and Mr. Roberts calls one team at a time. Gabby's team gets called first. They walk to the front of the room.

"Our game is called Bug In!" Gabby says. Then she looks at Carol,

who holds up a poster with super-cool magazine cutouts and drawings.

"You play the game as a bug, and your job is to *bug* people!" Carol explains.

This makes me laugh, and I tap Jasmine and Lily with my finger.

"Posey should've been on *that* team," I whisper. "He's an expert at bugging people, so he'd win every time!"

My friends giggle, and I know Posey overheard, but I'm kind of glad because it's kind of true.

"I never meant to *bug* you," Posey whines. "I only wanted an adventure."

His poor attempt at an apology doesn't make me want to forgive him. Instead, it unleashes my anger.

"It's not an adventure if it ruins everything!" I whisper sharply. Luckily, the next team is now talking, so I can continue my rant without getting caught.

"Just look what you've done, Posey! First you perform magic *in class*. Then you put glitter-litter in my classmate's bag, which ends up all over me. *And then* you invite the entire World of Make-Believe to lunch without asking me and they take over the entire playground!"

Posey hangs his head sadly.

But I don't care because I'm so much madder than mad. "And on top of everything, you *ruined* our presentations in

the library! Posey, I *never* want you to come back to school again!"

I fold my arms to see what Posey has to say about that. And I watch as tears roll down his cheeks. Jasmine and Lily pat Posey on the shoulder.

"Easy, Daisy," says Lily. "I don't think he meant to get us into trouble."

"Well, he didn't try *not* to get us in trouble, either," I say with a huff. "Now we have no report to present the nothing project that we couldn't do, and we're all going to fail!"

Posey looks at me through watery eyes. "Is there *anything* I can do to fix this, Daisy?"

I take a deep breath. "Not unless you can stop time and fix this whole mess!"

Posey's face suddenly brightens. "Hey, maybe there *is* something I can do to help!" he says.

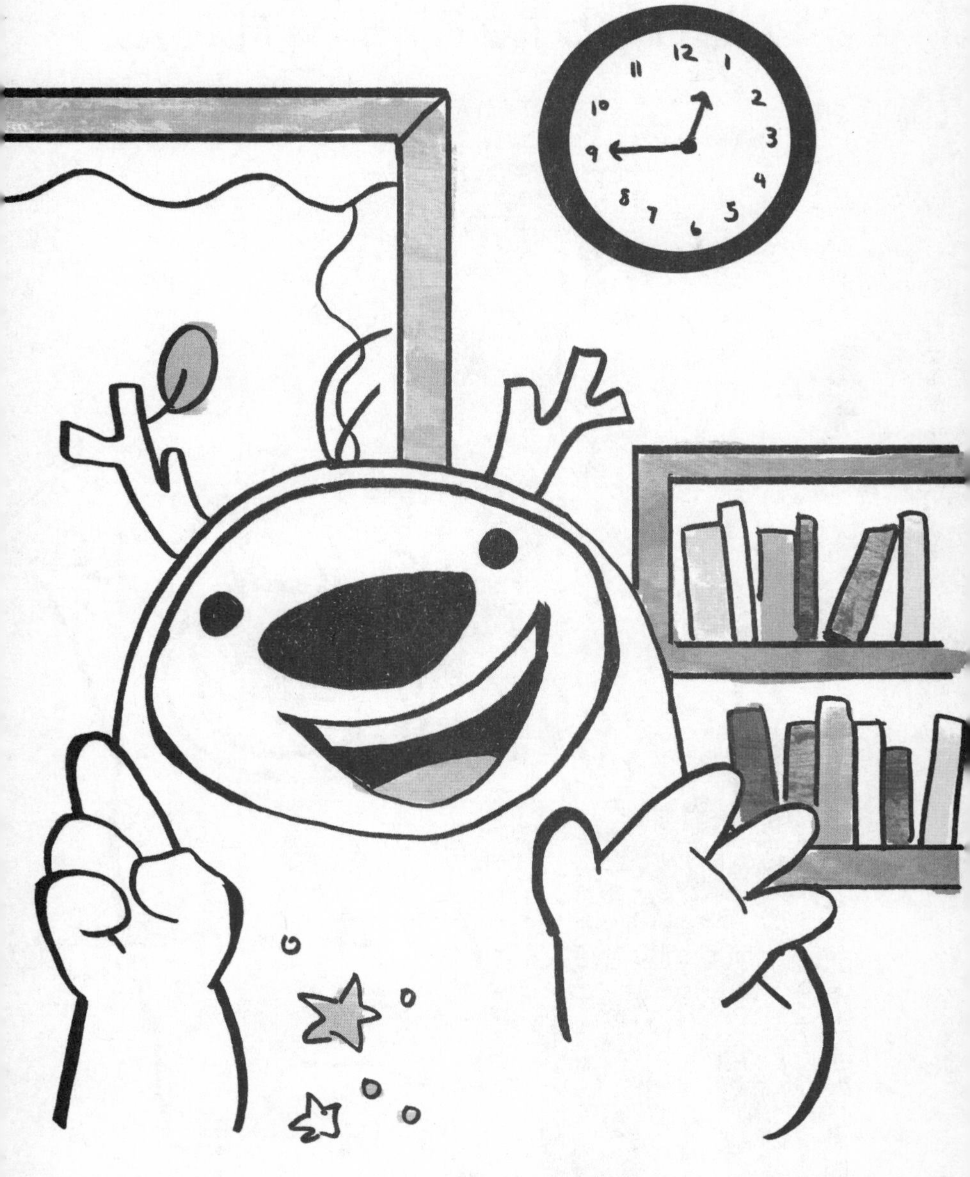

☆ Chapter Eight ☆

The Posey Pause

Mr. Roberts begins to call on our team, and right in the middle of what he's saying, Posey waves his hands.

SHWOOM!

Mr. Roberts freezes midsentence.

I look around and notice that the whole class is frozen! Gabby froze blowing a bubble with her gum. Wren froze halfway through a yawn.

John froze picking his nose. Jasmine, Lily, Posey, and I are the only ones *not* frozen.

"What's going on, Posey?" I ask, pointing at all the statues that were once my classmates.

"I call this trick the Posey Pause!" he says triumphantly. "We now have five minutes to fix whatever needs fixing!"

"Only *five* minutes?" Lily says, setting the timer on her watch. "We better get moving!"

I jump right in because I know exactly when our assignment went wrong. "It all started when that fairy appeared out of thin air!"

Lily shakes her head. "No, no, no!

It really started when we were arguing about what our video game should be about. *That's* why Posey made the fairy appear in the first place. He was trying to help us agree on a topic!"

Okay, I'll give Posey that one because it is actually true, I think.

"And Posey only planted the glitter-litter in Gabby's bag because Gabby and Carol were spying on us," Jasmine points out.

A twinge of guilt bubbles up inside me. *Jasmine's right about that, too, I think.*

"And they were only spying on us because they were suspicious," Lily adds.

Jasmine nods. "And they were only suspicious because *we* were fighting. If we hadn't wasted so much time arguing, maybe we wouldn't have even needed to go to the library, and then Posey wouldn't have ruined our work!"

All this reasoning makes me slump in my chair. It also makes me feel like a slimy, horrible, lowly Daisy Dreamer. Hmm, maybe even more like a Daisy Nightmare. I think I might owe Posey a big fat apology—like right now.

"I am *so*, *so* sorry I blamed you for everything, Posey," I cry out. "Can you ever forgive me?"

Posey looks at the table for a second and then back at me. "It's okay, Daisy," he says gently. "We all make mistakes . . . even imaginary friends. Lucky for you, though, I'm just as good at forgiving people as I am at going on adventures!"

This makes me feel better—that is, until Lily holds up her watch.

"Guys, our five minutes is almost up and we still don't have anything to present for our video game!"

We all stare at Mr. Roberts, who is still frozen in midsentence. I run through our options in my head. Magic is definitely out because I think we can all agree that there should be

no more magic at school today. And
that leaves us with only one other
option.

Lily's watch starts to beep.

"It's time to come clean!" I say.

CHAPTER NINE

HICCUP!

In a flash, Mr. Roberts finishes his sentence and it's our team's turn. We drag our feet to the front of the room and get ready to present a whole lot of nothing.

"Umm . . . ," Lily begins, and then looks at Jasmine.

"Uh—uhh . . . ," Jasmine stammers, and turns to me.

"Well . . . ," I say, stalling, not

wanting to say anything either.

Then somehow Jasmine finds words. "The truth is," she begins, "working as a team is hard. Our team had so many good ideas that we found it tough to pick just one."

Jasmine's right. We did have a lot of good ideas, I think. And that gives me a giant fairy–skateboard–stuffed animal idea! I nudge Jasmine and interrupt her.

"Which is *why* . . . ," I continue,

"we realized that having a bunch of different ideas could make the best video game of all!"

I turn to my friends and whisper, *"Follow my lead!"* Then I turn back to the class.

"When something unplanned happens in a video game, we call it a glitch or a hiccup. So we decided to call our game Hiccup! It's a video game that jumps around to tell the story from different points of view. Here's how to play. Lily, will you start by telling the class your game idea?"

Lily walks to the front, and I let her take over. "Our game starts with a fairy who wants to save her stuffed animals from an evil giant, but she needs some help."

Then I snap my fingers and yell, "HICCUP!"

Lily jumps back and I take over the video game! "Now there's a magical skateboard that wants to help the

fairy find her lost stuffed animals.
Together, they use the skateboard's
magical powers to sneak around the
giant."

Jasmine shouts, "HICCUP!"

The class all starts to giggle whenever we yell "hiccup" . . . because "hiccup" is a very funny word.

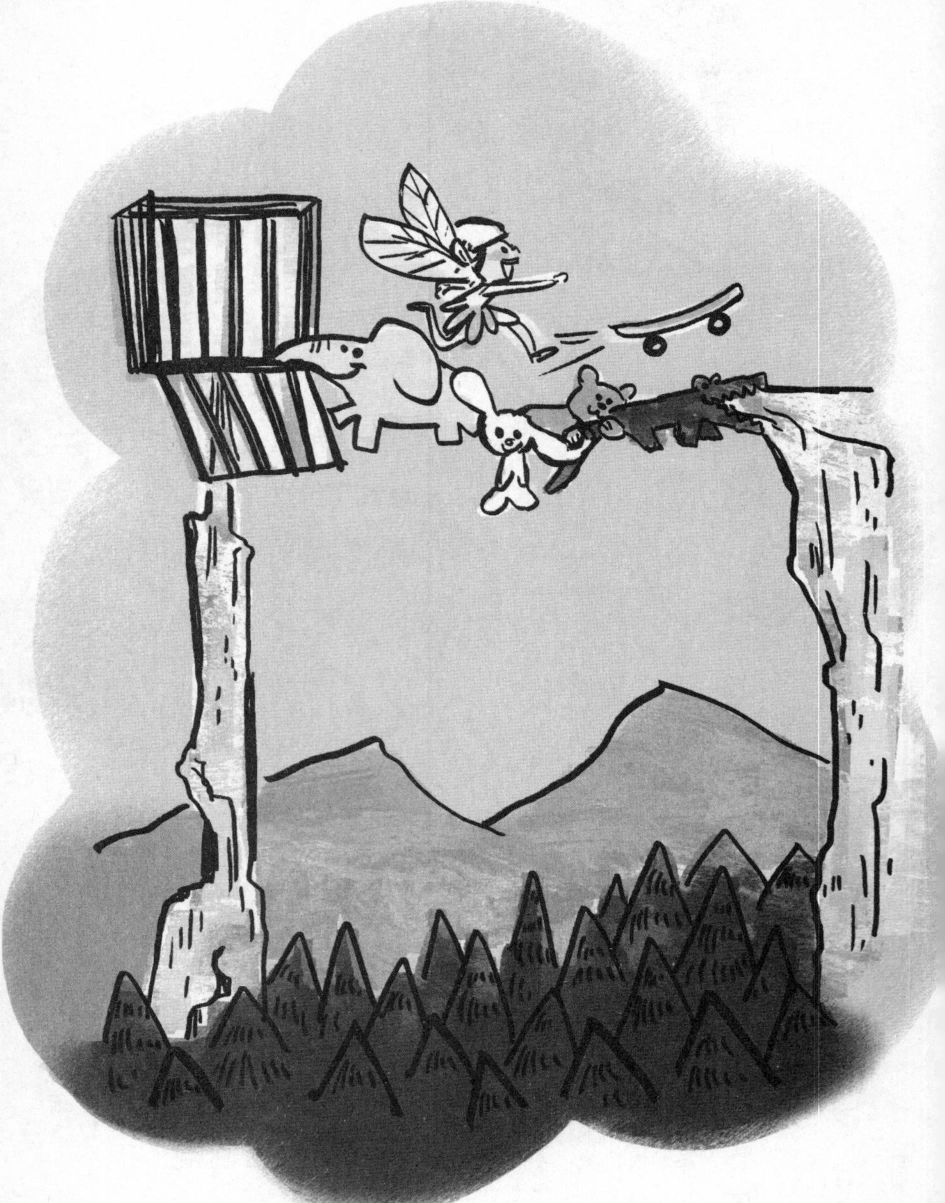

Jasmine continues, "But when the fairy and the skateboard find the stuffed animals, the giant captures them, too. So the stuffed animals have to work together to free all of them! And that's our game!"

The whole class claps, and I can hear Posey whistling in the back of the room. Hiccup! was here to stay.

☆ Chapter Ten ☆

Pretend Friends on the Loose

Believe it or not, everyone in class is playing Hiccup! now. Lily, Jasmine, and I wrap our arms around Posey and give him a great big thank-you squeeze.

"Posey, you can come to school with us anytime!" I say.

Then Jasmine and Lily give me a major *look*.

"Okay, okay—maybe not anytime

too soon . . . ," I add. And we all burst out laughing. That's when Mr. Roberts whistles through his fingers. The class gets quiet and sits back in their seats.

"We still have *one* presentation to go!" he says.

The final team of Jordan, Marcus, and Rico walks to the front of the room.

"Our game is called Pretend Friends on the Loose," Rico begins. Then Jordan turns over the group's poster board so everyone can see it.

Lily, Jasmine, and I gasp as Rico continues. "Our main character is called Rosy."

He points to a character that looks just like Posey! Which is why we're in total *shock*.

"In order to win the game, Rosy has to go around the playground, catching all the Pretend Friends in a big bag. It looks like this." Then Rico pretends to grab imaginary people

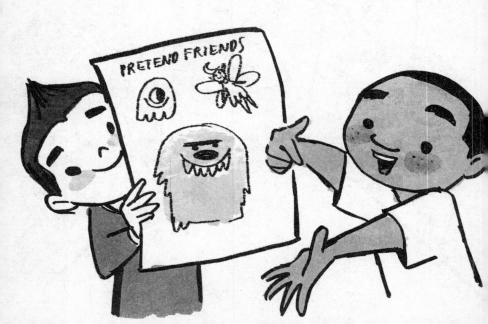

and put them back into his pretend big bag.

At this point we almost fall off our chairs because the Pretend Friends look like all of Posey's WOM buddies from the playground! The boys even made a map of the playground with trails for Rosy to catch the Pretend Friends.

Then Jasmine, Lily, and I turn all six of our eyes on Posey.

He scratches his head thoughtfully. "That's weird. . . . I *thought* I made everyone look like real-world kids!" Then he gulps and says, "Are you mad at me again, Daisy?"

And of course I'm mad. "I'm mad that we didn't think of Pretend Friends on the Loose for *our* game!"

Then I pull Posey close and tell him I'm only joking.

"Really?" he says, and I nod like crazy. Sure, Posey might be the best class pest, but he's also the best pretend friend in the whole world.

Check out Daisy Dreamer's next adventure!

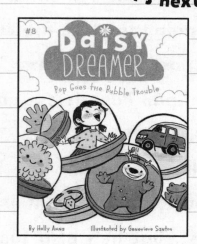

#8

Daisy DREAMER

Pop Goes the Bubble Trouble

By Holly Anna   Illustrated by Genevieve Santos

SPLAT!

I turn around just in time to see an orange tumble off the tippy-top of the orange pile and sploosh all over the floor.

That's the *third* one in two minutes!

Mom and I are at the grocery

store—one of the best places in the world. *Obviously.* Who doesn't love food?

But something keeps knocking the fruit over. And it's not me! I *pinkie swear*!

Just in case, I steer extra clear of the bananas.

KER-SPLAT! KER-SPLUNK!

Across the aisle, two peaches splatter to the floor like juicy yellow fruit bombs. And that's when I see him, sitting on top of the peaches like a little purple monkey with antlers.

"Posey!" I whisper loudly. "What are you doing up there?"

"Shopping!" he shouts with a big

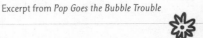

sticky grin. He hops down from the pile in one giant leap, knocking over more fruit. Peach juice drips from his chin.

"These samples are *amazing*!" he says, grabbing an apple and taking a huge bite.

"Those aren't samples!" I tell him, taking the apple out of his hand. "They are for sale. You have to pay for them first!" *Obviously.*

"Oh," he says, looking a little disappointed. "But I'm hungry!"

I roll my eyes. "You should never go to the grocery store hungry. It makes you want to eat everything!"

Excerpt from *Pop Goes the Bubble Trouble*

Then I swivel the cart around and catch up with Mom. She's moved to the cereal aisle.

"Ooh, Imagination Crunch!" Posey shouts, spying a rainbow-colored cereal box. He throws it into the cart. I quickly take it out and shove it back on the shelf.

"Daisy," Mom questions when I turn back around, "why are there Gooey Roll-Ups in our cart?"

I grab the Gooey Roll-Ups and put those back too. "Sorry, Mom!" I turn and wag my finger at my imaginary friend.

Excerpt from *Pop Goes the Bubble Trouble*